THE COMPLETE CHANSONS
Chansons . . . Livre premier . . . (1589)

RECENT RESEARCHES IN THE MUSIC OF THE RENAISSANCE

James Haar and Howard Mayer Brown, general editors

A-R Editions, Inc., publishes six quarterly series—

Recent Researches in the Music of the Middle Ages and Early Renaissance,
Margaret Bent, general editor;

Recent Researches in the Music of the Renaissance,
James Haar and Howard Mayer Brown, general editors;

Recent Researches in the Music of the Baroque Era,
Robert L. Marshall, general editor;

Recent Researches in the Music of the Classical Era,
Eugene K. Wolf, general editor;

Recent Researches in the Music of the Nineteenth and Early Twentieth Centuries,
Rufus Hallmark, general editor;

Recent Researches in American Music,
H. Wiley Hitchcock, general editor—

which make public music that is being brought to light
in the course of current musicological research.

Each volume in the *Recent Researches* is devoted
to works by a single composer or to a single genre of composition,
chosen because of its potential interest to scholars and performers,
and prepared for publication according to the standards that govern
the making of all reliable historical editions.

Correspondence should be addressed:

A-R EDITIONS, INC.
315 West Gorham Street
Madison, Wisconsin 53703

RECENT RESEARCHES IN THE MUSIC OF THE RENAISSANCE • VOLUME LX

André Pevernage

THE COMPLETE CHANSONS

Chansons . . .
Livre premier . . .(1589)

Edited by Gerald R. Hoekstra

A-R EDITIONS, INC. • MADISON

ANDRE PEVERNAGE
THE COMPLETE CHANSONS

Edited by Gerald R. Hoekstra

Recent Researches in the Music of the Renaissance

Library of Congress Cataloging in Publication Data:

Pevernage, André, 1542 or 3–1591.
    [Chansons, livre 1er]
    Chansons—livre premier— (1589)

    (The complete chansons / André Pevernage ; [v. 1])

    (Recent researches in the music of the Renaissance, ISSN
0486–123x ; v. 60)
    For superius, quinta, contratenor, tenor, and bassus.
    French or Latin words, principally sacred.
    Edited from the 1st ed. published: Chansons d'André
Pevernage. Livre premier : contenant chansons spirituelles à
cinq parties. A Anvers : De l'imprimerie de Christophe
Plantin, 1589.
    Words also printed as text with English transla-
tions: p.
    Includes bibliographical references.
    1. Chansons, Polyphonic.   2. Part-songs, Sacred.
3. Part-songs, French.   I. Hoekstra, Gerald R.
II. Series: Pevernage, André, 1542 or 3–1591.
Chansons ; v. 1.   III. Series: Recent researches
in the music of the Renaissance ; v. 60.
M2.R2384   vol. 60   [M2092]   83-3764
ISBN 0-89579-183-8 (set)
ISBN 0-89579-184-6 (v. 1)

Contents

Preface

Our conception of the Netherlandish chanson in the later decades of the sixteenth century rests primarily on the pieces of a few prominent composers, the most well known among these being Roland de Lassus (1532–1594) and Jan Pieterszoon Sweelinck (1562–1621), whose works are available in modern editions.[1] However, even though Lassus was born and trained in the Netherlands, he spent most of his life elsewhere, and the cosmopolitan styles of his chansons exhibit French and Italian traits as well as Netherlandish characteristics. Unlike Lassus, Sweelinck worked in the Netherlands throughout his life, and thus his chansons might be more accurately viewed as Netherlandish than those of Lassus. The few chansons of a third Netherlander, Philippe de Monte (ca. 1521–1603), that are available in modern editions contribute further to our picture of the late-sixteenth-century Netherlandish chanson;[2] but de Monte, like Lassus, spent most of his life outside the Netherlands, and his chanson output is much smaller than his production of madrigals. Therefore, even with the works of these three composers in modern editions, the lack of such editions of music by their contemporary countrymen has caused our picture of the later Netherlandish chanson to remain far from complete.

Indeed, a significant number of other composers working in the Low Countries had music published during the last third of the sixteenth century; among these composers are Noel Faignient (d. ca. 1595), Severin Cornet (ca. 1530–1582), Corneille Verdonck (1563–1625), and André Pevernage (1542 or 1543–1591). Pevernage was undoubtedly the most important among them, not only because he wrote a large number of chansons—eighty-three known pieces (counting *pièces liées* as single chansons)—but also because of the high quality of his music.

André Pevernage and His Music

André Pevernage published four books of chansons between 1589 and 1591 through the Antwerp firm of Christopher Plantin.[3] Except for three chansons that appeared in *Le Rossignol musical* (1597) and a single chanson in three *parties* included in the *Bici-*

nia, sive cantiones (1590), the pieces in these four books constitute Pevernage's entire output in the chanson genre. All of Pevernage's chansons, both from Plantin's publications and from *Le Rossignol* and the *Bicinia* are included in the present edition. Because the edition follows Plantin's publications of Pevernage's four books of chansons (referred to hereafter as Books I–IV) in organization and ordering of pieces, the seven Pevernage motets that appear in these source-prints are also included here. RECENT RESEARCHES IN THE MUSIC OF THE RENAISSANCE (hereafter RRRen) volumes LX–LXIV present Books I–IV, respectively. The chansons from *Le Rossignol* and the *Bicinia* are included at the end of RRRen volume LXIV. Each of these RRRen volumes contains an Introduction, Critical Notes, and Texts and Translations appropriate to the works included therein. This general Preface to the edition, on the other hand, appears only in the present RRRen vol. LX.

The four source-books of chansons came into print during the last years of the composer's life; he died in 1591 at the relatively young age of forty-eight. Pevernage was born in 1542 or 1543 in Harelbeke, a small town near Courtrai in the southern Netherlands.[4] The record of his initial appointment in 1563 as chapel master at St. Sauveur in Bruges lists him as "Andreas Pevernage de Harlebeca, clericus tornacensis," implying that he had served as a choirboy in Tournai during his youth. His stay in Bruges lasted less than a year. In October of 1563, Pevernage became chapel master at Notre Dame in Courtrai.

Popular rebellion and political upheaval disrupted life in the southern Netherlands during the 1560s and 1570s. These were the years during which Calvinist ideas spread rapidly through the area, and since, in the eyes of many of the people, the Roman Catholic church and the oppressive Spanish government were allied, religious dissent spread with political dissent. The rebellion and iconoclastic raids on churches that began in West Flanders in 1566 left Courtrai in miserable shape, and in 1578 Pevernage and his family were forced to flee to Antwerp. But that city cannot have been much better off, since its access to the sea had been cut off by the

Sea Beggars (revolutionary pirates allied with the Protestant cause), who controlled Holland and Zeeland at this time. Little is known of Pevernage's life from 1578 until 1584, when he returned to his post in Courtrai. Alexander Farnese, the new governor appointed by Philip II, had recaptured most of Flanders and Brabant by that time, and Courtrai had already been returned (in 1581) to the king, and thus to the Roman Catholic church.

During his tenure as chapel master in Courtrai, Pevernage composed a great deal. In addition to performing the duties required by his ecclesiastical position, he participated in the St. Cecilia Guild, a fraternity of wealthy, music-loving businessmen. The chapel master provided music for many of the activities of this society, and in 1569 the Guild named him *vicarius perpetuus*, a title that probably carried with it a stipend. Pevernage's first published works date from 1568—four of his motets found their way into a volume of the *Novi thesauri musici*, a collection of sacred music written by leading composers of the day, and printed by Antonio Gardano of Venice.[5] In 1578 more of Pevernage's motets were published; in fact, an entire volume of his motets and *elogia*, entitled *Cantiones aliquot sacrae*, was issued from the presses of Jan Bogard of Douai. During the 1580s a number of Pevernage's madrigals were included in volumes issued by Phalèse and Bellère in Antwerp. One of these volumes, *Harmonia celeste* (1583), was a collection of madrigals assembled by Pevernage himself. Although van der Straeten asserts that the composer traveled to Italy during the years preceding the publication of this collection, there is at present no documentation to support that claim.[6] A madrigal anthology like *Harmonia celeste* could easily have been assembled in the cosmopolitan city of Antwerp from music available there.

Only one year after his return to Courtrai, Pevernage was offered an appointment as chapel master at Notre Dame in Antwerp; this offer was probably the fruit of acquaintances made during his stay there. He accepted the position and moved back to that city, where he lived and worked for the remainder of his life.

Among his friends in Antwerp was the publisher Christopher Plantin, and, according to Stellfeld, Pevernage served Plantin as musical adviser.[7] Plantin's printing firm was one of the most important for music publishing in the Netherlands during the last quarter of the sixteenth century. Even though music constituted only a small part of Plantin's business, he took great care with the quality of his publications, and works by some of the leading musicians of his day, including Jacobus de Kerle,

George de la Hèle, Claude LeJeune, and Philippe de Monte, came off his presses. However, the publication of the four books of Pevernage chansons was one of Christopher Plantin's last personal contributions to music; indeed, an epitaph for Plantin in the first book of chansons relates that ''he died printing this work.'' Management of the Antwerp firm fell to Plantin's son-in-law, Jean Moretus (= Moerentorf), whose name appears on the title page of Book IV.

Pevernage's chansons were issued by the Plantin firm at a time when the polyphonic chanson was passing out of fashion in many circles. Yet the size of the four chanson books, the favorable record of sales extending into the seventeenth century,[8] and the release of a second edition by Phalèse in 1606 and 1607 all attest to the popularity these pieces enjoyed even at this late date.

The Four Books of Chansons

Pevernage's four books of chansons bear the following titles:

CHANSONS d'André Pevernage, Maistre de la chapelle de l'Eglise cathedrale d'Anvers. Livre premier, contenant chansons spirituelles à cinq parties. . . . A Anvers, De l'Imprimerie de Christofle Plantin. M.D.LXXXIX.

LIVRE SECOND des Chansons d'André Pevernage, Maistre de la chapelle de l'Eglise cathedrale d'Anvers. A cinq parties. . . . A Anvers, De l'Imprimerie de Christofle Plantin. M.D.XC.

LIVRE TROISIEME des Chansons d'André Pevernage, Maistre de la chapelle de l'Eglise cathedrale d'Anvers. A cinq parties. . . . A Anvers, De l'Imprimerie de Christofle Plantin. M.D.XC.

LIVRE QUATRIEME des Chansons d'André Pevernage, Maistre de la chapelle de l'Eglise cathedrale d'Anvers. A six, sept, et huict parties. . . . A Anvers, En l'Imprimerie Plantinienne, Chez la Vefve & Jean Mourentorf. M.D.XCI.

That Plantin would print four entire books of chansons by a composer who had so few pieces included in other collections of the time is not remarkable. Chanson anthologies had passed out of vogue during the 1560s, and during the last third of the century nearly all publishers favored volumes devoted to works of a single composer.

The organization of the four books clearly indicates that Pevernage conceived and planned them simultaneously. Three factors govern the arrangement of the chansons in the collection as a whole: the type of text—*spirituelle* or *profane*; the number of voices; and the modes. All of the *chansons spirituelles* are printed in the first book, and this special character of Book I is indicated on its title page. There are very few of the pieces in Book I that do not seem to warrant the designation *spirituelle*, and only two pieces of a devotional nature appear in the other volumes.[9] The majority of Pevernage's chansons are for five voices, and these fill his first three books. Book IV is reserved for chansons for six, seven, or eight voices. Within each source-volume, the pieces are grouped by mode (i.e., those in the same mode are placed together), but modal grouping does not extend from one volume to another. The bulk of each book is devoted to pieces with French texts. However, Books I, III, and IV conclude with devotional songs with Latin texts, many of which are prayers.[10]

The chanson books were printed in quarto format with partbooks labeled Superius, Contratenor, Tenor, Bassus, and Quinta. For the chansons with more than five voices, in Book IV, a single extra partbook was issued.[11] The voices in the Quinta and Sexta books do not maintain a consistent range from one piece to another. In some pieces they have the same tessitura as another voice; in others, these voices lie between two of the first four voices.

Many of the chansons are *pièces liées* (i.e., chansons consisting of two or more separate pieces, or *parties*).[12] Although each of the constituent pieces of a *pièce liée* ends with a strong cadence, they are linked harmonically. The constituent pieces are always in the same mode, and often, where there are only two *parties*, the first cadences on the dominant or subdominant, and the second begins at that pitch level and concludes on the tonic. *Pièces liées* were particularly popular among Netherlandish composers in the latter half of the sixteenth century. They offered composers a structural format for setting long texts in the expansive manner to which they were accustomed, while still maintaining formal coherence.[13]

In his own later edition of Plantin's four chanson books, Pierre Phalèse abridged the set. He printed Books I, II, and III as a single volume in 1606, and excluded from it all of the occasional chansons, the pieces with Latin texts, and a number of the *chansons spirituelles*. The pieces that Phalèse omitted from his edition are the following: Book I—nos. 2, 3, 4, 5, 7, 8, 9–10, 20, 25, 26–27, 28; Book III—nos. 16–21, 22, 23, 24. Phalèse copied the Plantin publication without change; even the occasional errors in the original remain uncorrected. A year later he reprinted Book IV as a separate volume, but this book he left intact, including in it all of the music.

Only one chanson from Plantin's original print appeared in a sixteenth-century vocal collection. This piece is *Resveillez vous chacun fidelle* (Book I, no.

14), which was printed in *Cinquante Pseaumes de David avec la musique à cinq parties d'Orlande de Lassus, Vingt autres Pseaumes . . . par divers excellens musiciens de nostre temps* (Heidelberg: Jerome Commelin, 1597). Two other works, *La nuict le jour* (Book IV, nos. 8–9), and the *Pater noster* of Book I (no. 28) were intabulated for lute by Emanuel Adriansen and appear in his *Novum pratum musicum* (Antwerp: Phalèse and Bellère, 1592).

A reliable and complete modern edition of Pevernage's chansons has long been needed. About half of them appear in a nineteenth-century series devoted to the history of Belgian music, *Trésor musical*, edited by. R.-J. van Maldeghem.[14] Most of these pieces were included in the issues of *Trésor musical* of 1869–1872. Maldeghem's series lacks the same chansons as the Phalèse edition of 1606, and it includes none of the chansons of Book IV. Thus, it seems fairly certain that Maldeghem worked from the Phalèse edition. Although Maldeghem provided a valuable service to his contemporaries by making this music available, he followed editing practices that are unacceptable to modern musicians and scholars. He altered the texts considerably and, in many cases, replaced the originals entirely with didactic or moralistic poems.[15] In a style in which text and music are so closely allied, such substitutions alter the character of the work and often force rhythmic changes in the music. Also, the constituent *parties* of several of the *pièces liées* appear separately, sometimes even in different issues of the series. Not only is the musical unity of the whole thus destroyed, but individual pieces ending on the dominant of the mode are left standing alone in the Maldeghem edition.

Complete sets of the partbooks of the Plantin edition of Books I–IV now reside in two libraries: the Bayerische Staatsbibliothek in Munich and the Österreichische Nationalbibliothek in Vienna. Incomplete sets are located in various other European libraries: the Bibliothèque du Grand Séminaire, Strasbourg (Book I, complete); the Gemeentemuseum, The Hague (Books II and III, S-C-B partbooks; Book IV, S-C-T-B partbooks); and the Archivo del Musica el Cabildo, Zaragoza, Spain (Book IV, T partbook only).

The *Bicinia, sive cantiones* and *Le Rossignol musical*

In RRRen volume LXIV, there are three chansons by Pevernage (*Si dessus voz levres de roses, Ma mignonne debonnaire,* and *Pour estr' aymé par grande loyauté*) from *Le Rossignol musical*, 1597, and one Pevernage chanson of three *parties* (*Deux que le trait d'amour*) from the *Bicinia, sive cantiones*, 1590. Complete copies of the *Bicinia* are held by the Augsburg Staats- und Stadtbibliothek and the Universitetsbiblioteket, Uppsala; another copy in the Paris Bibliothèque du Conservatoire is lacking some pages in the Superius partbook.

The only complete copy of *Le Rossignol musical* is the one in the Biblioteka Polskiej Akademii Nauk, Gdansk. A copy of the Tenor partbook, only, is held by the Universitetsbiblioteket, Uppsala. A set of the edition of 1598 lacking only the Quinta partbook is found in the Bibliothèque royale de Belgique, Brussels; a copy of the Quinta may be found in the collection of Westminster Abbey, London.

The Texts

After 1550, chanson composers began to select poetry of higher quality than did their predecessors, a tendency that Charles van den Borren suggests was due largely to the "winds of humanism that blew among them."[16] However, that many composers had set the poetry of Clément Marot as early as 1520 provides an important exception to this generalization that the texts chosen before 1550 were inferior to those used after that date. Marot's verse stands far above the general run of early chanson texts, which were dominated by the ubiquitous *chansons d'amours*. Although Marot's verse continued to be favored by musicians throughout the century, it was surpassed in popularity during the 1560s and 1570s by the poetry—especially the sonnets—of the *Pléiade* poet Pierre de Ronsard. Then, during the 1570s, composers turned to the works of Philippe Desportes and his contemporaries Amadis Jamyn and Antoine de Baïf for most of their texts. And by the mid 1580s, the poetry of these men had, in turn, been overshadowed by that of another generation.

In light of this succession of favorites among his contemporaries, Pevernage's taste in textual material seems puzzling at first. The numbers of poems set by him that can be attributed with confidence are as follows:

Clément Marot	18 poems
Philippe Desportes	10 poems
Pierre de Ronsard	3 poems
Mellin de St.-Gelais	1 poem
Guillaume Guéroult	1 poem
Jan van der Noot	1 poem

It seems surprising that Marot figures so prominently as a supplier of texts for Pevernage's chansons, which, presumably, were written during the thirty years preceding their publication between

1589 and 1591. While many of his contemporaries were issuing entire volumes devoted to settings of Ronsard's sonnets, Pevernage largely ignored the work of this poet, although he was undoubtedly familiar with it, and turned instead to Marot and Desportes. Pevernage's taste cannot simply be dismissed as backward just because he set so few texts by Ronsard; after all, Desportes also was fully Pevernage's contemporary.

That Pevernage should have found the style of Marot eminently suitable for musical setting is understandable. Marot had rejuvenated French poetry earlier in the century by abandoning the strict rules of the *Rhétoriqueurs* and espousing a lighter, simpler, less affected style. He favored the freedom, clarity, and lightness of folk poetry and contemporary Italian poetry. The content of Marot's verse is rarely deep or complex, since he shunned the "long-winded tirades on general topics and the classical themes of lyric poetry,"[17] and, according to A. J. Krailsheimer, "even where he has little or nothing to say, his craftsmanship usually enables him to write verse that is musical, witty, and gay."[18] The folk-like quality of Marot's verse was not accidental, but was carefully cultivated; incipits or refrains from fifteenth-century folk poems served as the starting point for many of his own chanson texts.[19]

Pevernage's preference for Desportes over Ronsard and the choice of those Ronsard texts that he did set is consistent with his taste for Marot. Desportes's style exhibits the same grace, fluency, and lack of complexity found in Marot's poetry. Although Ronsard did much to encourage musical settings of his poetry, his sonnets vary greatly in complexity, and thus in their suitability as song texts. Pevernage's choices in this respect tell us much about his poetic preferences. Two of the Ronsard texts that he selected are not sonnets, but poetic chansons (Book II, no. 9, and Book IV, no. 26), and the one sonnet he did set, *Ces deux yeux bruns* (Book III, nos. 7–8), ranks among the least complex examples of the genre. Furthermore, Pevernage set only the first eight lines of this sonnet, and he spread them over two *parties*. Thus, the picture that emerges from an examination of Pevernage's texts reveals a preference for poetry of lighter, simpler, and more "musical" qualities.[20]

The subjects of the chanson texts range from the devotional songs, prayers, and psalms of Book I to the songs that deal with the vicissitudes of love scattered throughout the other source-volumes. In the latter group of songs, such themes as the suffering and torment of unrequited love, the lover as servant, and the lover as captive occur repeatedly. The large number of humorous and epigrammatic verses about love manifest a fondness for witty maxims. Most of the humor comes from Marot; but it is from the poet's clever vein, not his bawdy one. Pevernage shunned the bawdy humor and tales of sexual adventure that were so popular with Lassus and some of the Parisians. Four of Pevernage's chansons have occasional texts. These include the epitaph for Christopher Plantin in Book I, an epithalamion for the governor of Courtrai in Book III, a song in praise of the city of Antwerp in Book IV, and an epitaph in honor of a Charles of Burgundy (see RRRen vols. LXIII and LXIV, Introduction), also in Book IV.

Pevernage's Musical Style

Although the style of Pevernage's chansons varies from piece to piece, some common features prevail throughout his compositions in this genre. The predominance of the Dorian, Phrygian, and Aeolian modes shows a distinct preference for the minor modes; indeed, only about one-third of the pieces are in major modes. Pevernage's harmonic writing is typical of its time: root position triads predominate, and dissonances are prepared. Although he avoided the extremes of his Italian contemporaries, Pevernage nevertheless introduced chromatic alterations liberally, even where they yield cross-relations. These alterations include not only changes of harmony above a constant root, as in the chord successions A major to A minor or D major to D minor, in which the thirds appear in different voices (see, e.g., Book I, no. 15, m. 28; Book II, no. 22, mm. 16–18; Book III, no. 14, m. 24), but also changes above a shifting root, as, for example, in the chord successions C major to A major or A major to F major (see, e.g., Book I, no. 17, mm. 2–4; Book II, no. 9, mm. 23–24). Such chromatic alterations allowed the composer to move easily in and out of the mode. Often they result from a madrigalistic interpretation of the text. More common than direct cross-relations are what might be called "spaced cross-relations," that is, cross-relations separated by an intervening harmony (see, e.g., Book I, no. 2, m. 3; Book III, no. 6, mm. 1–2; Book IV, no. 24, m. 53). Chromatic shifts within a single voice occur only infrequently, as at the beginning of no. 17 of Book I.

In most of Pevernage's chansons, the melodic dimension is subservient to the text. Except at points of imitation, the writing is often declamatory. Short fragments of text give rise to motives that are shaped more by rhythmic and harmonic exigencies than by concern for melodic development. Contra-

puntal and homophonic textures occur in relatively equal proportion, a distinct contrast with the predominantly contrapuntal style of such mid-century Netherlanders as Gombert and Clemens non Papa. Texture changes frequently in the chansons, since each phrase of text receives distinct treatment, and the choice of texture is often inspired by the rhythm or expression of the words.

Pevernage's rhythms also seem to be governed by the declamatory and expressive demands of the texts. The rapid syllabic declamation on minims (van den Borren calls it "quasi parlando") recalls the earlier Parisian style and the *note-nere* writing of the madrigal; however, Pevernage uses it in both the Ȼ meter with which it was first associated in the madrigal, and in the older ȼ.[21] Triple rhythms notated by coloration are rare in the chansons,[22] but Pevernage frequently introduced triple rhythms in the context of duple meter. He accomplished this with a regular alternation of minims and semiminims (♪♪ ♪ ♪♪ ♪) in passages of largely homorhythmic texture (e.g., in Book I, no. 1, mm. 19–20; Book IV, no. 6, mm. 15–16). In this edition, these triple rhythms are masked somewhat by the barring. The rhythmic effect of such passages recalls the musical settings of *vers mesuré a l'antique* produced by a number of Pevernage's French contemporaries, and Pevernage had probably encountered their works. However, triple rhythm patterns of this type also appeared frequently in mid-sixteenth-century madrigals (particularly those of Cipriano de Rore), and Pevernage was undoubtedly familiar with these, too.

Pevernage's familiarity with the style of the Italian madrigal is demonstrated not only by his attention to the rhythms of the text, but also by his concern for the pictorial and expressive dimensions of the poetry. Perhaps some of this sensitivity to the words was absorbed also from his contact with the music of Lassus. Madrigalisms underscore many words or phrases: sometimes they merely heighten the meaning; at other times they depict a word figuratively. Among the many instances of madrigal writing in the chansons, the following are cited as examples: the rapid melismatic flourishes on the word "rire" (Book I, no. 24), the close, syncopated imitation that depicts the "poursuivans ennemis" (Book I, no. 8), the quick motion in high voices that suggests the shimmering of quicksilver (Book III, no. 5), or the slowing rhythms, movement to lower tones, and suspensions for the word "mort" (Book I, no. 27; Book II, no. 21; Book III, no. 10).

The musical forms in Pevernage's chansons are what various scholars have called motet forms, through-composed forms, or evolutional forms.[23]

Each line, and sometimes each phrase, of text receives its own musical setting, appropriate to its rhythmic and expressive character. Repetition of music with new text occurs only rarely, as in *Susann' un jour* (Book I, no. 13) and *Resveillez vous* (Book I, no. 14), where preexistent melodies provide the impetus. The only other instances are found in *Les servans d'amour* (Book I, no. 23) and *Soyons plaisans* (Book IV, no. 25). In all four, the musical setting of the first two lines of text serves also for the third and fourth lines. Nine of the chansons have a repeated section at the end, but in every case both text and music are involved.[24]

Acknowledgments

The Bayerische Staatsbibliothek of Munich provided microfilm copies of the four books of Pevernage chansons published by Plantin; the Universitetsbiblioteket of Uppsala supplied a copy of the *Bicinia, sive cantiones*; and the Biblioteka Polskiej Akademii Nauk of Gdansk provided a microfilm of *Le Rossignol musical*. Much of the preparatory work for this edition was done during my doctoral study at Ohio State University. Thus, I owe a debt of gratitude to the graduate school for the University Fellowship granted me during this time; to the staff of the Ohio State Music Library and its former director, Olga Buth, for their generous help; and to Professor Richard H. Hoppin, who so thoughtfully encouraged and guided me in my work. Dr. William Huseman of the University of Oklahoma provided valuable advice regarding my translations of the French chanson texts; Dr. Derke Bergsma of Trinity Christian College, Palos Heights, Illinois, supplied translations of the Latin motet texts; and Dr. Patrick Kehoe of Wichita State University translated for me the Gheesdalius poem, *In musicam Andreae Pevernagii*, which appears in Book IV. To all of them I am grateful. I thank Möseler Verlag for permission to include in this edition seven pieces that appear in my volume of *Das Chorwerk* (No. 131, *André Pevernage: Sieben Chansons*). Thanks also to Oxford University Press and the editors of *Early Music* for their permission to include in this set my edition of *Bon jour mon coeur* (Book IV, no. 26), which appears in their publication, along with my article on the chanson (July 1980). Finally, thanks to Professor Howard Mayer Brown, general editor of the Recent Researches in the Music of the Renaissance series, for his prompt attention to my manuscripts and for his helpful criticism.

Gerald R. Hoekstra

Notes to the Preface

1. Lassus's chansons are found in Roland de Lassus, *Sämtliche Werke*, vols. XII, XIV, and XVI, ed. F. X. Haberl and Adolf Sandberger (Leipzig: Breitkopf & Härtel, 1894–1926). A few additional chansons appear in vol. I of Lassus, *Sämtliche Werke: Neue Riehe*, edited under the joint sponsorship of the Académie Royale de Belgique and the Bayerische Akademie der Wissenschaften, (1956–). For Sweelinck's chansons, see Jan Pieterszoon Sweelinck, *Werken*, ed. M. Seiffert et al. (Leipzig: 1895–1903). Although a new edition of Sweelinck's works, *Opera omnia* (1966–) is being issued by Vereniging voor Nederlandse Muziekgeschiedenis, the chansons have not yet been published.

2. Philippe de Monte, *Collectio decem carminum gallicorum alias Chansons françaises 4–5 vocum*, ed. G. van Doorslaer, Vol. XX of *Philippe de Monte: Opera*, ed. Charles van den Borren and Julius van Nuffel (1927–39; reprint, New York: Broude Brothers, 1965). The chanson volumes have not yet been issued in the *Phillippe de Monte: New Complete Edition*, ed. R. B. Lenaerts et al. (Louvian, 1975–).

3. The four books of chansons will be referred to here as Books I, II, III, and IV, according to their original order of publication. On Pevernage's chansons, see J.-A. Stellfeld, *Andries Pevernage: zijn leven—zijne werken* (Louvain: De vlaamsche Drukkerij, N.V., 1943); this study offers a thoroughly documented study of the composer's life and the publications of his music and includes appendices reproducing archival documents concerning Pevernage's life. See also Gerald R. Hoekstra, "The Chansons of André Pevernage (1542/43–1591)" (Ph.D. diss., The Ohio State University, 1975).

4. Stellfeld, *Andries Pevernage*, p. 8, cites information from the inscription on Pevernage's tomb indicating that he was forty-eight at the time of his death on 30 July 1591 and concludes that he was born in 1543. However, the composer might just as well have been born in 1542 after 30 July.

5. The *Novi thesauri musici* consists of five volumes of motets, all published in 1568. Pevernage's four motets appear in books II (one motet), III (two), and IV (one) of this publication.

6. See Edmond van der Straeten, *La musique aux pays-bas*

avant le XIXe siècle (1867–88; reprint, New York: Dover Publications, Inc., 1969), VI:56–57.

7. J.-A. Stellfeld, *Bibliographie des éditions musicales plantiniènnes* (Brussels: Publication de l'Académie royale de Belgique, [1949]), p. 135.

8. See Stellfeld, *Andries Pevernage*, Appendix XXVI, which shows records of sales from Plantin's journals, 1589–1595. Copies were shipped to Mons, Courtrai, Douai, Frankfurt, Bruges, Maestricht, and Cambrai, among other cities.

9. Those pieces that appear in Book I, but do not seem to be *chansons spirituelles* are nos. 5, 15, 26, and 27. Pieces of a devotional nature (in addition to the motets) found in other volumes are no. 1 of Book III and nos. 4 and 5 of Book IV.

10. Publications that included pieces in several languages were not unheard of in the late sixteenth century, although they were not common. Another example of this practice is the *Bicinia, sive cantiones* (Phalèse, 1590), which combines motets, madrigals, and chansons. In addition to the chanson mentioned earlier, Pevernage also has a madrigal in this collection.

11. The locations of the extra parts for the seven- and eight-voice pieces will be discussed in the Introduction to the edition of Book IV (see RRRen vols. LXIII and LXIV).

12. The French term "parties" is used here to refer to the constituent pieces of *pièces liées* (chansons consisting of two or more separate pieces), while the English "parts" is reserved for voice parts. Since *pièces liées* are, in a sense, single units, their numbers will be joined with an N-dash (e.g., nos. 26–27) in the discussions presented in this edition.

13. Most of Pevernage's motets consist of two *partes*.

14. The entire series has been reprinted: R.-J. van Maldeghem, *Trésor musical: Collection authentique de musique sacrée et profane des anciens maitres Belges*, 5 vols. (Vaduz, Leichtenstein: Kraus Reprint, Ltd., 1965). A complete listing of the chansons of Pevernage included in this collection is found on pp. 65–67 of Stellfeld, *Andries Pevernage*. Stellfeld's listing contains several mistakes: Book I, no. 6 is found in 1869, no. 4 (not 5); Book I, no. 15 appears in the issue of 1865, no. 9 (not 1869, no. 9); and Book II, no. 22 should be designated 1871, no. 3 (not 1870, no. 3).

15. For several examples, see Hoekstra, "The Chansons of André Pevernage," p. 25.

16. Charles van den Borren, "The French Chanson," *New Oxford History of Music*, Vol. IV: *The Age of Humanism, 1540–1630* (London: Oxford University Press, 1968), p. 21.

17. François Lesure, *Musicians and Poets of the French Renaissance*, trans. by E. Gianturco & H. Rosenwald (New York: Merlin Press, Inc., 1955), p. 23.

18. A. J. Krailsheimer, *The Continental Renaissance: 1500–1600* (Harmondsworth, Middlesex, England: Penguin Books, Ltd., 1971), p. 176.

19. See P. M. Smith, *Clément Marot: Poet of the French Renaissance* (London: The University of London, Athlone Press, 1970), p. 127. The notes accompanying the chansons in C. A. Mayer's edition of the *Oeuvres lyriques* (London: The University of London, Althone Press, 1964) offer numerous examples of such borrowing.

20. Further comments on the attributions of the texts are offered in the Introductions to the individual volumes of this edition.

21. James Haar furnishes the following description of *note-nere* writing: "Pieces written in this notation have the mensural sign $\mathbb{C}$ in contrast to the more typical $\mathbb{\phi}$ of the period. The note values are, on the whole, shorter, with much of the text declaimed on minims and semi-minims, and although the blackness of the page is not always striking, a *note-nere* madrigal is visibly darker than, say, a typical Verdelot madrigal." James Haar, "The *Note Nere* Madrigal," *Journal of the American Musicological Society* XVIII (1965): 23.

22. Only two instances occur: Book II, no. 18, and Book IV, no. 9.

23. The term "evolutional form" comes from Robert Trotter, "The Chansons of Thomas Crecquillon: Texts and Forms," *Revue belge de musicologie* XIV (1960): 56–71.

24. Book II, nos. 3, 9, 18, 21; Book III, nos. 4, 6, 18; Book IV, no. 18, and *Si dessus voz levres de roses*, from *Le Rossignol musical*. *C'est amour si rare*, the third *partie* of Pevernage's chanson in the *Bicinia, sive cantiones*, also has a repeated unit at the end, but the composer appended a new cadence to the second appearance.

Introduction

Chansons . . . Livre premiere . . . (1589)

The compositions of *Chansons . . .* (1589) (hereafter referred to as Book I) are grouped according to mode as follows:

nos. 1–5	Hypodorian on G
nos. 6–8	Hypoionian on F
nos. 9–14	Dorian on G
nos. 15–17	Ionian on F
nos. 18–19	Hypomixolydian on G
nos. 20–21	Phrygian on E
nos. 22–24	Hypoionian on C
no. 25	Hypodorian on D
nos. 26–27	Aeolian on D
no. 28	Dorian on G

This grouping appears to have little significance beyond the fact that pieces with similar ranges for their respective voice-parts appear together. The only exception to the modal grouping is the placement of *Pater noster* (no. 28); it is at the end of Book I, presumably because of its Latin text. In this discussion, modes of the pieces are determined by the range and ambitus of the Tenor, following the method prescribed by most sixteenth-century theorists for judging the modes of polyphonic compositions. The ambitus of the Superius generally lies an octave above the Tenor; the ambitus of the Contratenor lies an octave above the Bassus. All voices in pieces in the plagal modes lie generally a fourth below their counterparts in the authentic modes. The ranges of voice parts are fairly consistent within each modal group and correspond with the ambitus of either the authentic or plagal modes, with only one exception: the Tenor of no. 6 appears to be in the authentic rather than in the plagal mode, although the other voices are appropriate for a polyphonic piece in the plagal mode. Pevernage himself did not specify modes in Book I, and we have no evidence that he was familiar with and agreed with the system of twelve modes outlined by Glareanus (*Dodecachordon*, 1547) and Zarlino (*Istitutioni harmoniche*, 1558). However, a number of pieces in Pevernage's Books II, III, and IV are clearly in Aeolian on A, and thus it does not seem unreasonable to label nos. 26–27 of Book I as Aeolian on D, rather than Dorian with a flat. Furthermore, none of the

other pieces in Dorian on D has a flat in the key signature. That Pevernage, as well as other composers, saw Aeolian and Dorian as two distinct modes is clear from studies of their harmonic writing in various modes.[1]

Pevernage's Book I, a volume of *chansons spirituelles*, is dedicated, appropriately, to a member of the clergy, the "Tres Reverend Pere en Dieu, Monseigneur Pierre Simons, Evesque d'Ipre" (see Plate II for a facsimile of the dedication page):

> After considering the requests of some of my music-loving friends to bring into print this little work of mine, on which in times past I spent my youth, I knew of no one better to whom to dedicate it than you, my Lord. For, in addition to the singular favor accorded to Music and the masters of it, and the service that I owe you, it seems fitting to me. The subject is fitting for you, for it contains only spiritual songs, which I have separated from those that are secular, in order not to mix the earth with the heavens and not to offer you something that might offend your vocation. I ask you, then, that it please you, in memory of the good friendship shown to me for so long, to accept it with a hand as kind as the heart with which it is presented to you, and remember to honor me with your requests, if there is any way I can be of service. And now I will bring this to a close, my Lord, with my most humble request for your blessing, praying that God will give you a long and healthy life, full of all joys and blessings, physical as well as spiritual. Antwerp, 6 October 1589.
>
> Your very humble servant
> André Pevernage.

Until the invasion of the Sea Beggars (see Preface, p. viii) forced his departure from Ghent in 1578, Simons was canon of the cathedral there. He was then appointed as a priest of St. Martin's in Courtrai, but this church was plundered by the iconoclasts in that same year. According to Stellfeld, Simons was of great service to the people of Courtrai during this time of difficulty.[2] It was also at this time that the composer and the priest became acquainted. Simons's appointment as Bishop of Ypres came in 1583, and he still held that position when Pevernage's chansons were published.

Only seven of the texts for pieces in Book I can be

confidently assigned to particular poets. Of these, six are the work of Clément Marot, and one is by Guillaume Guéroult. Authorship of the remainder of the texts is unknown, although reasonable conjectures can be made for some of them. For instance, the text of the opening dedicatory prayer set in no. 1, *Je veux, mon Dieu, par musical' ardeur*, requesting God's blessing on the work, may well have been written by the composer himself. The text of another chanson, *Las, me faut il tant de mal supporter* (nos. 9–10), was first printed in the poetic anthology *La fleur de poésie françoyse* of 1543; the text appears anonymously there, but Stellfeld ascribes it to Guillaume Guéroult. Stellfeld also speculates that the *Epitaphe de Christofle Plantin* (nos. 26–27) may have been written by Jan van der Noot, a leading Flemish poet of the day and a friend of the composer.[3]

The poems of Marot set by Pevernage in Book I include two psalm-versifications, two prayers, a *rondeau*, and a *ballade*. It seems bold of the composer to publish settings of Marot psalm-versifications at a time when hostilities between Catholics and Protestants were still strong. Psalms in the vernacular had always been associated with the Protestant cause, although decrees against their use seem to have been treated with some ambivalence by the authorities.[4] That Pevernage would include them in a volume dedicated to a bishop shows that at least some Catholics had fully accepted psalm-versifications as appropriate for their own use. Pevernage borrowed not only the texts of Psalms 33 and 51, but also the Genevan tunes associated with them. In the setting of Psalm 33, *Resveillez vous chacun fidelle* (no. 14), the Genevan melody (see Example 1) appears as a straightforward *cantus firmus* in the Tenor.

Example 1.

Res- veil- lez vous cha-cun fi-del- le,   Me- nez en Dieu joy'
Lou- an- g'est tres se- ant' et bel- le   En la bou-che de

or- en- droit,   Sur la dou-ce har- pe   Pen- du
l'hom-me droit:

en es- char- pe   Le Sei-gneur lou- ez: De lutz, d'e- spi-

-net- tes   Sain- tes chan-son- net- tes   A son nom jou- ez.

The original melody of Psalm 51, *Misericorde au povre vicieux* (see Example 2), in contrast, dominates no

single voice in Pevernage's setting (no. 21), but enters freely in all five voices, particularly at short points of imitation.

Example 2.

Mi- se- ri-cor-de au po-vre vi- ci- eux,   Dieu tout puis-sant,

se- lon ta grand'cle-men-ce,   Us' à ce coup de ta bon-té

im- men- se,   Pour ef- fa-cer mon faict per-ni- ci- eux:

La- ve moy, Si- re, et re- la- ve bien fort,   De ma com-mis'

i- ni- qui- té mau-vai- se: Et du pe-ché qui m'a ren-

-du si ord,   Me net- toy-er d'eau de gra-ce te plai- se.

Although Huguenot melodies were associated also with Marot's two *Oraisons*, or prayers (set as nos. 18 and 19), they were not widely known, and of the nine composers who set this pair of texts, only Louis Bourgeois used these tunes.[5]

Another Marot poem, his *Chant de May* (Ballade XVIII; set as nos. 22–24 in Book I), provided the text for Pevernage's contribution to the popular stream of sixteenth-century celebrations of spring; this type of chanson is otherwise notably absent from Pevernage's *œuvre*. Each strophe of this poem receives independent musical treatment in Pevernage's three *parties*, although the single-line refrain of *partie 3* has the same musical setting as that of *partie 1*. Appropriate to the spirit of the text, the music for this song is brighter and more homorhythmic than most of the pieces in the volume.

The remaining text from Marot is the *rondeau Au bon vieux temps* (no. 15). Pevernage's setting of this nostalgic text, which looks back to a time when lovers were more sincere in their expressions of affection, seems out of place in a collection of *chansons spirituelles*.

Like the prayers and psalm-versifications, Guillaume Guéroult's text *Susanne un jour* (set in no. 13) is a product of the Protestant camp. Written for devotional use among Protestants and drawing on the apocryphal story of Susanna and the elders, the poem was first set by Didier Lupi, *secondi*, in 1548. This text was set numerous times by both Protestants and Catholics during the 1560s and 1570s.[6] Most of these settings, including Pevernage's, draw their melodic material from the Tenor of Lupi's setting. Lupi's melody (see Example 3) appears as the *cantus firmus* in the Tenor of Pevernage's version, although fragments infiltrate the other voices as well.

Example 3.

Su- san- n' un jour d'a- mour so- li- ci- té- e
Fut en son coeur tri- st' et des- con- for- té- e

Par deux viel- lards con- voi- tans sa beau- té, El- le
Voy- ant l'ef- fort fait à sa cha- ste- té.

leur dit: Si par_____ des loy- au- té De ce

corps mien vous a- vez jou- is- san- ce, C'est fait de moy

si je fay re- si- stan- ce, Vous me fe- rez mou- rir

en des- hon- neur: Mais j'ay- me mieux pe- rir en

in- no- cen- ce Que d'of- fen- ser par pe- ché le Sei- gneur.

*This note is G in Pevernage's setting.
**This note is B-natural in Pevernage's setting.

If, as Kennth Levy asserts in his study of the *Susanne* tradition, Catholics had abandoned the text by the 1580s because of its clear association with the Protestant cause,[7] it seems surprising that Pevernage would include this poem in a publication issued just a few years after Antwerp had been freed from the grip of the Protestants.

Book I contains another moralistic narrative chanson text that closely parallels *Susann' un jour* in many ways. The anonymous text, *Joseph requis de femme mariée* (set in nos. 11–12) recounts in verse the Old Testament story of Joseph, the young man who, in spite of the consequences, resisted the advances of Potiphar's wife. Considering the similarity of *Susann' un jour* and *Joseph requis* in subject matter, poetic structure, and opening musical motives, one might conjecture that the setting of the Joseph story was inspired by the *Susanne* tradition. No other settings of *Joseph requis* are known, however, and the lack of an apparently borrowed melody suggests that no tune was traditionally associated with this text.

The text of *Trois fois heureux et gracieux* (set in nos. 16–17) also has a Biblical origin. An anonymous and rather crudely constructed versification of the Beatitudes from Jesus' Sermon on the Mount (Matt. 5), this long poem is divided into two *parties* of roughly equal length. Some of the texts of the prayer-like chansons at the beginning of Book I (e.g., nos. 1–4, 6, and 8) also seem Biblical in character; they may well be conscious or subconscious paraphrases of scripture. The similarity of the chanson poetry to Biblical passages, particularly some of the Psalms, may result from the fact that the authors of these texts faced many of the same problems in the hostile atmosphere of the sixteenth-century Netherlands that were faced by the Psalmists in Biblical times.

The one occasional chanson in Book I, the *Epitaphe de Christofle Plantin* (nos. 26–27), is also one of the more madrigal-like chansons in the volume. With melismas extending the words "Pleurez Muses," declamatory settings of the exclamation "Las," and slowly resolving suspensions on "il est mort," this work demonstrates the composer's sensitivity to the expression of the text. There are other even more madrigal-like chansons in the later volumes of this edition.

The *Pater noster* setting that closes Book I resembles Pevernage's motets more than his chansons. Longer note values and polyphonic textures predominate. Although occasional syllables are set to minims, the *quasi-parlando* declamatory style found in many chanson phrases is lacking.

Editorial Commentary

This edition of the *Chansons . . . Livre premier . . .* (1589) is based on the complete set of partbooks in the Bayerische Staatsbibliothek of Munich (shelf number Mus pr 32), which was made available to the editor on microfilm. Brackets enclose all editorial additions and alterations in the music.

Only three of the chansons in Book I bear titles in the original publication: the *Consecration de la table* (no. 18); the *Action de graces* (no. 19); and the *Epitaphe de Christofle Plantin* (nos. 26–27). All other titles in this edition consist merely of the incipit of the text and have been added, but not bracketed, by the editor. The original numbering of the chansons has been retained, but Arabic numerals are substituted for the Roman figures of Plantin's edition. Although the Plantin publication gives the designation "*2. partie*" or, in the case of no. 24, "*3. partie*" at the heads of the subsequent chansons in the *pièces liées*, its counterpart, "*1. partie*," does not appear at the beginning of the first chanson of such groups. Thus, in this edition, the designation "*1. partie*" has been added where appropriate. One unusual *pièce liée* deserves special comment. The *première partie* of *Joseph requis de femme mariée* (no. 11) concludes with a semibreve, a semibreve-rest, and a single barline, rather than with the usual longa and double bar. Its mate (no. 12) bears the designation "*Suitte*," rather than the more usual "*2. partie*." Pevernage apparently intended the performer to continue into the *seconde partie* without a pause.

No problems of text underlay were encountered by the editor, largely because Pevernage's style is predominantly syllabic, and also because Plantin was very careful with text placement in his publications. All repetitions of text in Plantin's print were either written out or indicated by the sign *ij*; the *ij* text has been written out and bracketed here. No additional editorial repetitions of text were necessary. The parentheses around "je pri'" in *Je veux, mon Dieu, par musical' ardeur* (no. 1) are found in the source.

Except in those cases described below, spelling and punctuation of the text remain unaltered in this edition. All abbreviations, including ampersands, have been written out, and archaic spellings with "u," "v," and "i" have been changed where they might confuse the modern reader, as, for instance, in *ie viure (je vivre)*. The use of contractions and apostrophes to indicate elisions follows the source. Accents have been added to vowels where they were omitted from the source (either by mistake or because accent-usage was not standardized) and where their absence might affect pronunciation or confuse the reader. Otherwise, spellings have not been modernized, even though it is thought that the pronunciation, with a few exceptions, should not differ substantially from modern French. The most frequently encountered archaism is the obsolete "s," shown in the following examples, where the form appearing in the underlaid text of Plantin's print is compared with the appropriate modern form: *preste* = *prête*; *esjouir* = *éjouir*; *escharpe* = *écharpe*; *estre* = *être*; and *maistre* = *maître*. Most au-

thorities agree that in the sixteenth century, these words were pronounced like their modern counterparts, but that orthography had not yet caught up with pronunciation.[8] In this edition, syllable-divisions indicate whether the "s" is to be pronounced or not: where the "s" falls before the division, it is silent; where it falls after the division, it must be pronounced. For example, in *mais-tre* and *pres-te* the "s" is silent; in *e-spe-ran-ce* and *de-sor-don-né*, the "s" is pronounced. Another common archaism is seen in spellings with "oi," where modern French has "ai," as in *regnoit* (*regnait*), *resistoit* (*resistait*), or *apparoistre* (*apparaître*). Again, the modern "ai" sound should be used.

Punctuation follows the source for the most part, but frequent editorial changes were made for the sake of clarity. In many cases, the punctuation following a phrase of text in the source is not clear because the final appearance of the phrase is indicated with the *ij* sign and thus includes no punctuation. Full stops (usually indicated in the edition with a colon) were added where the comma used in the source seemed insufficient, or where a colon was lacking in the source because the phrase of text makes its last appearance by means of a repeat sign.

The editorial incipit for each piece gives the name, clef, key signature, mensuration sign, and first note of each part as found in Plantin's print. For the G- and moveable C- and F- clefs of the source, this edition uses the treble-clef, tenor G-clef, and bass clef. Although its name has been retained, the placement of the Quinta voice varies from piece to piece, depending on its range. Where the range of the Quinta corresponds to that of the Superius, it is placed on the fourth staff from the bottom. Where its range is like that of the Tenor, it appears on the middle staff. Ranges of all voices are indicated immediately before the modern clefs. (Performers should note that the range does not always give a reliable impression of the tessitura; for instance, the bottom note of the specified range may appear only once or twice in a given work, and the most common low note in the piece may otherwise be a fourth above that indicated in the range-finder.)

Note values have been reduced by half, except for the final note of each piece, which is a longa in the original and has been transcribed here as a whole-note with a fermata. Pevernage used only two meter signatures, ¢ and C, with no apparent distinction in musical styles. Whether the composer intended a different meaning for the two signs is uncertain; nevertheless, they have been retained.

Of course, the barlines in this edition are intended only to serve as an aid to eyes accustomed to modern notational practice, and, thus, they should not affect the rhythmic performance of the music. Remembering this is particularly important when performing sections where quarters and eighths alternate to produce a triple rhythm that, with barring, looks more like a passage of syncopation. (See e.g., Book I, no. 16, mm. 12–15.)

Accidentals are editorial if written above the staff, and from the source if written within the staff. Editorial accidentals have been supplied sparingly, and consideration has been given to general sixteenth-century practices as well as to Pevernage's obvious taste for cross-relations and fluctuations between major and minor forms of a chord. Where sharp signs in the source cancel flats, they have been changed to naturals in the edition. In the source, an accidental is valid only for successive notes of the same pitch, unless the second statement of that pitch begins a new phrase, in which case the validity of the accidental is not always clear. In the source, an accidental is canceled either by a rest or by an intervening note of a different pitch, and this system is also followed here, since it seems clearest in music with such frequent and temporary pitch alterations—and thus accidentals that are redundant in modern practice are nevertheless preserved here. Both original and editorial accidentals should be considered valid for consecutive notes within measures. Where previously inflected pitches recur after intervening notes and the accidental must be invalidated, an editorial reminder is provided above the staff.

The extreme care, frequency, and consistency with which Pevernage supplied accidentals are noteworthy and make the volumes issued by Plantin unusual for their time. Where a performer would expect to alter a tone by the rules of *musica ficta*, the composer has already supplied the appropriate accidental. However, Pevernage did make one notable departure from general sixteenth-century practices in that he avoided the diminished harmony in first inversion for the penultimate chord at cadences (i.e., dim. VII⁶–I). Although he invariably supplied a sharp to the third where the penultimate chord lies a fourth below the cadence chord (and where anyone familiar with the style would add one anyway), he consistently left unaltered those penultimate chords that have roots a major second below the cadence chord and in which the cadence is approached by 2–1 motion in the lowest voice (see, e.g., no. 28, mm. 13–14). Pevernage's consistency in this matter suggests he intended the VII⁶ to remain unaltered. His general thoroughness and consistency in marking accidentals make it doubtful that he intended the performer to add many accidentals of his own.

The few ligatures that appear in the original print are marked with horizontal brackets (⌐⌐) here. Although Pevernage did use coloration for triplets in other books of the series published by Plantin, none appears in the *Chansons . . . Livre premier . . .* (1589).

Critical Notes

The source volume is clearly printed and relatively free from error. The following notes list the discrepancies, all of which are minor, between the present edition and Pevernage's *Chansons . . . Livre premier . . .* (1589).

No. 4—M. 33, Superius, note 3 has a sharp.

No. 6—The incipit, "Seigneur," is printed at the beginning of the Contratenor, Tenor, and Bassus parts.

No. 10—M. 6, Tenor, last note has a sharp sign that functions as a cautionary natural.

No. 11—Last note in all parts is a semibreve in the source, rather than the customary longa; see the Editorial Commentary above.

No. 13—M. 57, Superius, first note has a sharp sign that functions as a cautionary natural.

No. 14—M. 9, Quinta, note 4 has a sharp in the source, apparently an error since it results in conflict with the other voices.

Notes to the Introduction

1. See Gerald R. Hoekstra, "The Chansons of André Pevernage (1542/43–1591)" (Ph.D. diss., The Ohio State University, 1975), pp. 68–71, and the discussions of the harmonic profiles of various modes in Robert M. Trotter, "The Franco-Flemish Chansons of Thomas Crecquillon" (Ph.D. diss., University of Southern California, 1957), and Andrew Haigh, "The Harmony of Palestrina" (Ph.D. diss., Harvard University, 1946). The contents of the latter are summarized in Haigh, "Modal Harmony in the Music of Palestrina," in *Essays in Honor of Archibald T. Davison* (Cambridge, Mass.: Harvard University Press, 1957).

2. J.-A. Stellfeld, *Andries Pevernage: zijn leven—zijne werken* (Louvain: De vlaamsche Drukkerij, N.V., 1943), p. 63.

3. Ibid., p. 60. Stellfeld's ascription appears in the text of his book without documentation. However, in his list of contents for Pevernage's Book I, he lists the source only as *Fleur de Dame* (1548), a later anthology in which the poem ap-

peared, and he does not ascribe the poem to Guéroult. The title is given without author in the listing of contents for *La Fleur de poésie* by Frédéric Lachèvre in his *Bibliographie des recueils collectifs de poésies du XVIᵉ siècle* (Paris: Edouard Champion, 1922).

4. A decree of 1562 explicitly forbade singing the Psalms in the Netherlands; see Orentin Douen, *Clément Marot et le Psautier Huguenot* (Paris: Imprimérie nationale, 1878), I: 1. Just two years later, Plantin published an edition of the Marot-De Beze psalms with the king's permission. However, in 1570 this work was included in an index of forbidden books that was printed by Plantin himself.

5. See Howard Slenk, "The Huguenot Psalter in the Low Countries: A Study of its Monophonic and Polyphonic Manifestations in the 16th Century" (Ph.D. diss., The Ohio State University, 1965), p. 194.

6. Kenneth Levy cites thirty-three settings that span an entire century. See Levy, " 'Susanne un jour': The History of a 16th-Century Chanson," *Annales musicologiques* I (1953): 375–408.

7. Levy apparently did not realize that Pevernage was Catholic, since he writes that "the only *Susanne*s . . . composed late (i.e., after ca. 1580 . . .) were the work of non-Catholic composers." Ibid., p. 385, note.

8. E.-J. Bourciez, *Phonétique française* (Paris: Editions Klinksieck, n.d.) gives an historical overview of French pronunciation. See also Jeannine Alton and Brian Jeffery, *Bele Buche e Bele Parleure: A Guide to the Pronunciation of Medieval and Renaissance French for Singers and Others* (London: Tecla Editions, 1976).

Texts and Translations

The following translations were made by the editor with the helpful advice and guidance of Dr. William Huseman of the University of Oklahoma at Norman. They are for the most part literal and follow the structure of the verse.

Chansons . . . Livre premier . . . (1589)

No. 1

Je veux, mon Dieu, par musical' ardeur,
Chanter chansons au los de ta grandeur;
Car en toy gist le but de mon courage:
Mais comme rien ne peut sortir de moy,
Qui soye bon sans estr' aydé de toy,
Preste ta main (je pri') à cest ouvrage.

(I would, my God, with musical ardor
Sing songs in praise of your greatness;
For in you lies the longing of my heart:
But since nothing good can come from me
Without having been aided by you,
Place your blessing, I pray, on this work.)

No. 2

C'est toy, Seigneur, c'est toy sans plus Seigneur,
Qui fais aux tiens ceste grac' et faveur,
Qu'alors qu'ils sont pretz d'aller en ruine,
Tu les soustiens et les gardes de cheoir:
Puis leur ouvrant les yeux, tu leur fais veoir
Qu'un tel secours vient de ta main divine.

(It is you, Lord, the Lord above all,
Who gives to your own this grace and favor,
That when they are about to take the path of destruction,
You sustain them and keep them from falling:
Then, opening their eyes, you make them see
That such help comes from your divine hand.)

No. 3

En toy doncques, ô Dieu, en toy tout seul Seigneur,
Je mettray desormais tout l'espoir de mon coeur,
Laissant aux reprouvez leurs vaines confiances.

Heureux qui faict en toy ses desirs de mourer:
Heureux qui peut en toy ses desseings asseurer:
Heureux qui en toy seul fonde ses esperances.

(In you, then, O God, in you alone, Lord,
I will henceforth put all the hope of my heart,
Leaving to the damned their vain confidence.
Happy is he who places his desires in you,
Happy is he who can fulfill his designs in you,
Happy is he who places his hopes in you alone.)

No. 4

O Seigneur Dieu, qui vois ma passion,
Ne me delaiss' en cest' affliction:
Chasse ton ire, adouci ton courage,
Vueill' en douceur ta colere changer:
Tens moy la main, sauve moy du danger,
Qui m'est prochain par ce cruel orage.

(O Lord God, who sees my suffering,
Do not abandon me in this affliction;
Dispel your anger, soften your heart,
Grant that your wrath change into gentleness:
Extend to me your hand, save me from the danger
That approaches in this cruel turmoil.)

No. 5

Quand je voy tout le monde rire,
C'est lors que seul je me retire,
A part en quelque lieu caché,
Comme la chaste Tourterelle,
Perdant sa compagne fidelle,
Se branche sur ung tronc seiché.

(When I see everyone laughing,
That is when I retire alone,
Hidden in some secret place,
Like the chaste turtledove,
Upon losing her faithful companion,
Perches herself on a dead tree.)

No. 6

Seigneur, j'ay mis entente,
Ferm' espoir et attente

En toy tant seulement,
Dont mon am' esperdue
Ne sera confondue
Perpetuellement.

(Lord, I have put my thoughts,
Sure hope, and expectation
In you alone;
Therefore, my bewildered soul
Will not be eternally
Confounded.)

No. 7

A mon Dieu maintenant je me veux presenter;
Je veux bas à ses pieds tout en pleurs me jetter,
Poussant du fond du coeur ceste voix lamentable:
J'ay peché devant toy, pere doux et clement,
Je m'appelle ton fils, mais c'est indignement;
Mon malheur ne merit' un nom si favorable.

(I would present myself to my God now;
I would throw myself down at his feet in tears,
Raising from the bottom of my heart this lamentable
    voice.
I have sinned before you, gentle and mild father;
I call myself your son, but do so unworthily;
My wretchedness does not merit such a favorable
    name.)

No. 8

O Seigneur Dieu mon esperance,
Donne moy pleine delivrance
De mes poursuivans ennemis,
Puis que chez toy pour asseurance
Je me suis à refuge mis.

(O Lord God, my hope,
Give me full deliverance
From the enemies that pursue me,
For I have taken refuge in you
For my safety.)

No. 9 [1. partie]

Las, me faut il tant de mal supporter,
Sans que personn' en ayt la cognoissance,
Faisant semblant tousjours me contenter,
Et si n'ay plus de mon bien esperance.

(Alas, I have to bear so much pain
Without anyone knowing about it;
I always make a semblance of being contented
And no longer have any hope of happiness.)

No. 10   *2. partie*

Oste moy doncq, mon Dieu, la souvenance
De ce malheur auquel ne puis pourvoir;
Ou me donnez si longue patience,
Qu'aultre que vous ne le puisse sçavoir.

(Take from me then, my God, all traces
Of this affliction, which cannot be sustained;
Or give me such enduring patience,
That no one else will know about it.)

No. 11   [*1. partie*]

Joseph requis de femme mariée
Pour s'esjouir de son corps à plaisir,
Fut fort constant de coeur et de pensée,
Craignant du tout en si grand mal perir.

(Joseph, asked by a married woman
To take her body for his pleasure,
Was constant in heart and mind,
Fearing that such great evil would bring his ruin.)

No. 12   [*2. partie*]

Car nullement n'a voulu obeir,
Ayant de Dieu la crainte pour defence:
Ains resistoit, gardant la consequence,
Que le peché desplaist au grand Seigneur:
Abandonant son manteau par science,
Est devenu de l'amour le vainqueur.

(For in no way did he want to follow her wishes,
Having fear of God as his defense:
Thus he resisted, being mindful
That sin displeases the Lord.
Wisely abandoning his cloak,
He became the conqueror of love.)

No. 13   Guillaume Guéroult

Susann' un jour d'amour solicitée
Par deux viellards convoitans sa beauté,
Fut en son coeur trist' et desconfortée,
Voyant l'effort fait à sa chasteté.
Elle leur dit: si par desloyauté
De ce corps mien vous avez jouissance,
C'est fait de moy si je fay resistance,
Vous me ferez mourir en deshonneur:
Mais j'ayme mieux perir en innocence
Que d'offenser par peché le Seigneur.

(Susanna, solicited for love one day
By two old men coveting her beauty,
Was sad of heart and discomforted,
Seeing the attempt made at her chastity.

She said to them: If by perfidy
You take pleasure from possessing my body,
I am dead if I resist,
You will kill me in dishonor:
But I would rather die in innocence
Than offend the Lord by sin.)

No. 14   Clément Marot

Resveillez vous chacun fidelle,
Menez en Dieu joy' orendroit,
Louang' est tres seant' et belle
En la bouche de l'homme droit:
    Sur la douce harpe
    Pendu' en escharpe
  Le Seigneur louez:
    De lutz, d'espinettes,
    Saintes chansonnettes
  A son nom jouez.

(Awake, all ye faithful,
Rejoice in God now and forever,
Praise is fitting and good
In the mouth of the righteous:
    On the sweet harp
    Hanging from the shoulder
  Praise the Lord.
    On lute, on spinet,
    Play holy songs
  To his holy name.)

No. 15   Clément Marot

Au bon vieux temps un train d'amour regnoit
Qui sans grand art et dons se demenoit;
Si qu'un bouquet donné d'amour profonde,
C'estoit donné toute la terre ronde;
Car seulement au coeur on se prenoit.

(In the good old days a manner of love prevailed
That was carried out without great style and talent,
So that a bouquet given in deep love
Was like giving the whole round world;
For only for the heart did one reach.)

No. 16   [1. partie]

Trois fois heureux et gracieux
Sont les pauvres sans erre,
Pour ce qu'à ceux sont les hauts cieux:
Heureux vous debonnaire,
Car à vous est la terre:
Heureux ames pleurantes,
Vous serez bien plaisantes:
Heureux vous qui sans vice
Desirez la justice,
Vous serez abondantes.

(Thrice happy and blessed
Are the lowly poor,
For theirs are the heavens above;
Happy are you meek,
For to you is the earth:
Happy the souls that mourn;
You will be comforted.
Happy are you who without vice
Desire justice;
You will be filled.)

No. 17   2. partie

Heureux ô brave bande,
Qui fais misericorde,
Misericorde grande
Nostre Dieu vous accorde:
O nette conscience,
Vostre Dieu vous verrez:
Heureux qui par clemence
Sont paisibles trouvez,
Ils seront enfans de Dieu nommez:
Et qui seuffrent par gens iniques,
Ceux là tiendront en fin les lieux celiques.

(Blessed, o good people
Who show mercy;
Great mercy
May our God show to you.
O spotless conscience,
You will see your God:
Blessed are they who by mercy
Are found to be peace-loving,
They shall be called the children of God.
And those who suffer by the hand of the wicked,
To them shall be granted heavenly places in the
    end.)

No. 18   Clément Marot

Consecration de la table

O souverain pasteur et maistre,
Regarde ce troupeau petit,
Et de tes biens seuffre la paistre
Sans desordonné appetit:
Nourrissant petit à petit
A ce jourd'huy ta creature,
Par celuy qui pour nous vestit
Un corps subjet à nourriture.

(*Table Blessing*)

(O sovereign shepherd and master,
Look on this little flock

And of thy goodness suffer it to eat
Without inordinate appetite.
Nourish thy creature
Little by little today
Through him who for us took upon himself
A body subject to nourishment.)

No. 19   Clément Marot

Action de graces

Per' eternel, qui ordonnez
N'avoir soucy du lendemain,
Des bien que ce jour nous donnez,
Te mercions de coeur humain.
Or puis qu'il ta pleu de ta main
Donner au corps menger et boire,
Plaise toy du celeste pain,
Paistre nos ames à ta gloire.

(*Thanksgiving*)

(Eternal Father, who commands us
Not to worry about the morrow,
For the good things which you give us today
We give you thanks from our human hearts.
Now as it has pleased you to give from your hand
Food and drink for the body,
So may it please you to give heavenly bread
On which our souls may feast for your glory.)

No. 20

O Seigneur dont la main toutes choses enserre,
Per' eternel du tout, qui m'as formé de terre,
Qui rens par ton pur sang nos pechez nettoyez,
Et qui feras lever mon corps de pourriture,
Entens mes tristes cris jusqu'au ciel envoyez,
Et prens pitié de moy, qui suis ta creature.

(O Lord, whose hand enfolds all things,
Eternal Father of all, who formed me of earth,
Who cleanses our sins by your pure blood,
And who will raise my body from corruption,
Hear the sorrowful cries I send up to heaven
And take pity on me, thy creature.)

No. 21   Clément Marot

Misericorde au povre vicieux,
Dieu tout puissant, selon ta grand' clemence,
Us' à ce coup de ta bonté immense,
Pour effacer mon faict pernicieux:
Lave moy, Sire, et relave bien fort,
De ma commis' iniquité mauvaise:
Et du peché qui m'a rendu si ord,
Me nettoyer d'eau de grace te plaise.

(Grant mercy to this poor and depraved one,
All powerful God, according to thy great mercy,
Grant at this moment of thy great goodness
To blot out my pernicious deed.
Wash me, Lord, and cleanse me thoroughly
Of the great iniquities I have committed,
And of the sin that has made me so unclean,
Please cleanse me with the water of grace.)

No. 22   [*1. partie*]   Clément Marot

En ce beau mois delicieux,
Arbres, fleurs et agriculture,
Qui durant l'hyver soucieux
Avez esté en sepulture,
Sortez pour servir de pasture
Aux troupeaux du plus grand pasteur!
Chascun de vous, en sa nature,
Louez le nom du Createur!

(In this beautiful, delightful month,
Trees, flowers, and all growing things
That have been buried
During the tiresome winter
Come out to serve as pasture
To the flocks of the greatest shepherd!
Let each of you, according to his nature,
Praise the name of the Creator!)

No. 23   *2. partie*

Les servans d'amour furieux
Parlent de l'amour vain' et dure,
Où vous, vrays amans curieux,
Parlez de l'amour sans laidure.
Allez au champs sur la verdure
Ouyr l'oyseau, parfait chanteur;
Mais du plaisir, si peu qu'il dure,
Louez le nom du Createur!

(The slaves of unbridled love
Speak of a love vain and cold,
While you, true and earnest lovers,
Speak of a love that is not unseemly.
Go to the fields on the green meadow
To hear the bird, perfect singer;
But for that pleasure, however briefly it lasts,
Praise the name of the Creator!)

No. 24   *3. partie*

Quand vous verrez rire les cieux
Et la terr' en sa floriture,
Quand vous verrez devant vos yeux
Les eaux luy bailler nourriture,
Sur peine de grand' forfaicture

Et d'estre larron et menteur,
N'en louez nulle creature:
Louez le nom du Createur!

(When you see the skies laugh
And the earth in its flowering,
When you see before your eyes
The waters give it nourishment,
At the risk of committing a great crime,
And of being a thief and a liar,
Do not praise any creature for it:
Praise the name of the Creator!)

No. 25

Veu les ennuys qu'il y a en ce monde,
Plaisir ce n'est d'y vivre longuement:
Estre vaut mieux en la vie seconde,
Où est sans fin joyeux contentement:
Console doncq ton trist' entendement
Par la raison, homme Chrestien, et pense
Que vous aurez heureuse recompense
De tout le bien qu'aurez faict icy bas,
Dieu tout puissant, par sa bonté immense,
Vous a promis un eternel soulas.

(Given the troubles that are found in the world,
There is no pleasure in living here long;
Of much greater value is the second life,
Where one has joyous contentment without end.
Therefore, console your sad thoughts
By use of reason, Christian man, and remember
That you will have happy recompense
For all the good that you do here below.
Almighty God, by his immense goodness,
Has promised you eternal solace.)

No. 26   [1. partie]

Epitaphe de Christofle Plantin

Pleurez Muses, pleurez, attristez vos chansons,
Regrettans le trespas d'un de vos nourrissons,
L'industrieux Plantin, le premier de nostr' aage.

(Epitaph for Christopher Plantin)

(Weep, Muses, weep; darken your songs
To mourn the passing of one whom you nourished,
The industrious Plantin, the best of our age.

No. 27   *2. partie*

Qui n'a rien espargné d'argent, n'y pein' aussi,
Pour rendre vostre los par le mond' esclarcy,
Las! Muses, il est mort, imprimant cest ouvrage.

(Who never spared money or effort
To offer your praises to the world in full splendor;
Alas, Muses, he died printing this work.)

No. 28

Pater noster qui es in celis:
Sanctificetur nomen tuum:
Adveniat regnum tuum:
Fiat voluntas tua sicut in celo et in terra:
Panem nostrum quotidianum da nobis hodie:
Et dimitte nobis debita nostra,
    sicut et nos dimittimus debitoribus nostris:
Et ne nos inducas in tentationem:
Sed libera nos a malo.
Amen.

(Our Father, who art in heaven,
Hallowed be thy name:
Thy kingdom come,
Thy will be done on earth
    as it is in heaven.
Give us this day our daily bread
And forgive us our debts
As we forgive our debtors.
And lead us not into temptation,
But deliver us from evil.
Amen.)

CHANSONS
D'ANDRE' PEVERNAGE,

MAISTRE DE LA CHAPELLE
DE L'EGLISE CATHEDRALE
D'ANVERS.

LIVRE PREMIER,
contenant Chansons spirituelles
à cincq parties.

A ANVERS,

De l'Imprimerie de Christofle Plantin.

M. D. LXXXIX.

Plate I. André Pevernage: *Chansons . . . Livre premier . . .* (1589)
Superius partbook, title page.
(Bayerische Staatsbibliothek, Munich)

A TRESREVEREND
PERE EN DIEV,
MONSEIGNEVR PIERRE
SIMONS, EVESQVE D'IPRE.

 E S T A N T *deliberé à la follicitation de plufieurs mes amys amateurs de la Muficque, de mettre en lumiere ce mien petit ouurage, du quel le temps paßé i'ay exercé ma ieuneße : Ie n'ay fceu à qui mieux le dedier qu'à vous,* MONSEIGNEVR. *Car outre ce que la finguliere faueur que portés à la Muficque, & profeßeurs d'icelle, & le feruice que ie vous doys, m'y femondent, le fubiect vous eft propre, pour ne contenir autres que* Chanfons Spirituelles, *que i'ay voulu feparer de celles qui font prophanes, à fin de ne mefler la terre auec les cieux, & ne vous offrir chofe qui puiße offenfer voftre vocation. Ie vous prie doncques, qu'il vous plaife, en memoire de la bonne affection que de long temps m'auez monftré, l'accepter d'außi bonne main, comme de bon cœur il vous eft prefenté; & vous refouuenir de me honorer de vos commandemens, s'il s'offre en quoy ie vous puiße faire feruice. Et ce pendant ie conuertiray la fin de ceftes,* MONSEIGNEVR, *en mes treshumbles recommandations à vos beneuoléces: Priant Dieu, vous donner, en longue & faine vie, multiplication de toutes felicitez & benedictions, tant corporelles que fpirituelles. En Anuers le* VI. *d'Octobre,* M. D. LXXXIX.*

Voftre treshumble feruiteur

André Peuernage.

Plate II. André Pevernage: *Chansons . . . Livre premier . . .* (1589)
Superius partbook, dedication page.
(Bayerische Staatsbibliothek, Munich)

Plate III. André Pevernage: *Chansons . . . Livre premier . . .* (1589)
Superius partbook, opening page of no. 2, *C'est toy, Seigneur.*
(Bayerische Staatsbibliothek, Munich)

CHANSONS . . . LIVRE PREMIER . . . (1589)

1. Je veux, mon Dieu, par musical' ardeur

2. C'est toy, Seigneur

6

3. En toy doncques, ô Dieu

4. O Seigneur Dieu, qui vois ma passion

5. Quand je voy tout le monde rire

6. Seigneur, j'ay mis entente

26

7. A mon Dieu maintenant je me veux presenter

30

8. O Seigneur Dieu mon esperance

34

9. Las, me faut il tant de mal supporter

10. Oste moy doncq, mon Dieu

40

11. Joseph requis de femme mariée

12. Car nullement n'a voulu obeir

48

13. Susann' un jour

52

14. Resveillez vous chacun fidelle

54

15. Au bon vieux temps

16. Trois fois heureux et gracieux

17. Heureux ô brave bande

18. Consecration de la table

70

19. Action de graces

[Clément Marot]

74

20. O Seigneur dont la main

21. Misericorde au povre vicieux

[Clément Marot *Psaume 51*]

10
Dieu tout puis- sant, [Dieu tout puis- sant,]
Dieu tout puis- sant, [Dieu tout puis- sant,] se- lon ta grand'
-vre vi- ci- eux, Dieu tout puis- sant, Dieu tout puis-sant, se- lon ta grand'
vi- ci- eux,] Dieu tout puis- sant, se- lon ta grand'
- eux,] Dieu tout puis- sant, Dieu [tout puis- sant,] se- lon ta grand'
15
se- lon ta grand' cle-men- ce, U- s'à ce
cle-men- ce, se- lon [ta grand' cle-men- ce,] U- s'à ce coup, [U- s'à ce
cle-men- ce, se- lon [ta grand' cle-men- ce,] U- s'à ce coup
cle-men- ce, U- s'à ce coup, [U- s'à ce
cle-men- ce, U- s'à ce coup, [U- s'à ce
20
coup de ta bon- té, de ta bon- té im- men- - se, Pour
coup] de ta bon- té, de ta bon- té im- men- se,
de ta bon- té im-men- se, de ta [bon- té im- men- se,] Pour
coup] de ta bon- té, de ta bon- té im- men- - se, Pour
coup] de ta bon- té, [de ta bon- té] im- men- se, Pour

22. En ce beau mois delicieux

[Clément Marot]

86

23. Les servans d'amour furieux

[Clément Marot]

24. Quand vous verrez rire les cieux

96

25. Veu les ennuys qu'il y a en ce monde

26. Epitaphe de Christofle Plantin

27. Qui n'a rien espargné

28. Pater noster